THE GOOD, THE BAD & THE GASSY

by Annie Auerbach

mang**chapters**

visit us at www.abdopublishing.com

Reinforced library bound edition published in 2009 by Spotlight, a division of ABDO
Publishing Group, 8000 West 78th Street, Edina, Minnesota 55439. This edition
reprinted by arrangement with TOKYOPOP Inc. www.tokyopop.com

Author	Annie Auerbach
Illustrator	Mike Norton
Design and Layout	Erika Terriquez
Cover Design	Anne Marie Horne
Senior Editor	Nicole Monastirsky
Digital Imaging Manager	Chris Buford
Pre-Press Supervisor	Lucas Rivera
Art Director	Anne Marie Horne
Production Manager	Elisabeth Brizzi

Library of Congress Cataloging-in-Publication Data

This title was previously cataloged with the following information:
Auerbach, Annie.
  The good, the bad, and the gassy / written by Annie Auerbach ; illustrated by Mike
Norton.
    p. cm. -- (The Grosse Adventures ; bk. 1)
  Summary: After a field trip to the science museum, eight-year-old twins Stan and
Stinky Grosse build a rocket for the fourth-grade Astronomy Fair, but when it fails to
take off they employ their favorite hobby--farting--in an attempt to beat Penelope and
win first prize.
  [1. Rockets (Aeronautics)--Fiction. 2. Science--Exhibitions--Fiction. 3. Flatulence--
Fiction. 4. Brothers--Fiction. 5. Twins--Fiction. 6. Schools--Fiction. 7. Humorous
stories.] I. Norton, Mike, ill. II. Title.
PZ7.A9118Goo 2006
[Fic]--dc22   2006016454

For Dan,
who still thinks farts are funny.

—A.A.

CONTENTS

BONUS MANGA

JOURNEY TO URANUS

CHAPTER ONE
IT'S A JUNGLE OUT THERE

Deep in an unexplored region of South America, Stinky and Stan hack their way through the dangerous jungle . . .

CAW-CAW!

EE-EE-OO!

LET'S SEE WHAT'S UP HERE.

OHHHHH . . . !

IT'S THE LOST TEMPLE OF—

STINKY! STAN! TIME FOR DINNER!

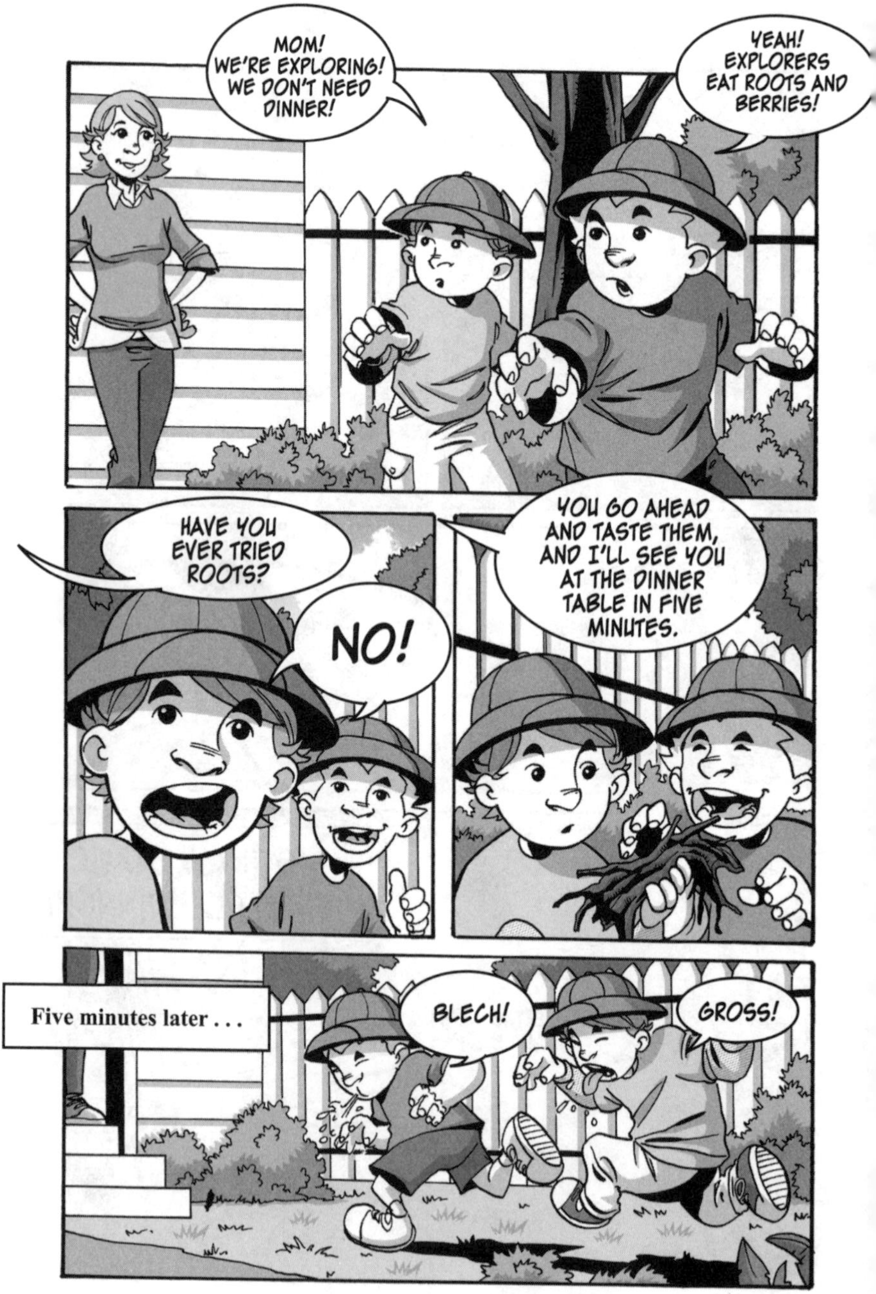
MOM! WE'RE EXPLORING! WE DON'T NEED DINNER!
YEAH! EXPLORERS EAT ROOTS AND BERRIES!
HAVE YOU EVER TRIED ROOTS?
NO!
YOU GO AHEAD AND TASTE THEM, AND I'LL SEE YOU AT THE DINNER TABLE IN FIVE MINUTES.
Five minutes later . . .
BLECH!
GROSS!

Stinky and Stan Grosse were two of the most curious brothers you'd ever want to meet. South America? Antarctica? You name it and they wanted to see it.

Even though they were fraternal twins, they were really quite different. Stan was the type to jump out of a plane barefoot, with a fuzzy idea of where he might land. Stinky would not only know the exact coordinates of where they would land, he would also bring an extra pair of shoes for Stan.

No matter what they were doing, Stinky and Stan had the best time when they were together. Their dream was to one day explore every part of the world.

But at the moment, they were exploring the ultimate frontier—the fourth grade.

CHAPTER TWO

SILENT BUT VIOLENT

The next morning, all the kids in Stinky and Stan's fourth-grade class gathered together on the sidewalk next to the school bus. It was field trip day, and you know how exciting that can be! Their teacher, Miss Mulch, was taking them to the Burbsburg Science Museum to learn about planets, stars, black holes, and more.

"This is going to be really cool!" Stan said to Stinky.

"I hope you're right," Stinky replied.

"How could it *not* be awesome?" asked Stan. "It's going to be all about space."

Stinky nodded and then added, "Just remember our last field trip. The Sewage Treatment Plant was awful."

"Hmm," said Stan. "You're right. That *was* awful! It took days for my nose to recover from the smell!" Then Stan

brightened. "But remember: *any* field trip beats sitting in class all day!"

Stinky smiled. "That's a good point," he said.

Just then, Miss Mulch tried to get everyone's attention. "Everyone form a single file line!" the teacher called out.

The kids scrambled to form a line— everyone except Grñpæk Yvlåöqçkn, who wasn't paying attention. He was a foreign exchange student who could *understand* English, but couldn't *speak* a word of it.

"That means you, too, Grrr— Grnn—," began Miss Mulch. She couldn't pronounce the student's name. No one could.

Miss Mulch called to Stinky, who was nearby, to help out. He pulled Grñpæk into line and the students began to board the bus.

When Stan climbed aboard, he headed to the back of the bus. He took a seat next to Eugene Clunkenheimer.

"Hey, Eugene," said Stan.

"Hey, *a-a-a—*" began Eugene.

"Take cover!" yelled Stan. He shielded his face with his arms. All you could see was his spiked hair peeking out.

"*—chooo!*" sneezed Eugene. When he recovered from what seemed like the world's biggest sneeze, Eugene replied, "Hey, Stan."

There wasn't a day that went by that Eugene didn't sneeze. In fact, there wasn't an hour that went by that he didn't sneeze. In fact, there wasn't a—well, you get the picture.

"What's that?" Stan asked him, pointing to a sheet of paper in Eugene's hands.

"It's for Miss Mulch. It's a new list of the things I'm allergic to," replied

Eugene, blowing his always-stuffed-up nose with a tissue.

Stan took a look at the list.

From the desk of
DR. MELONHEAD

for Eugene Clunkenheimer

- Grass
- Pollen
- Dirt
- Mold
- Flowers
- Cheese
- Venus Fly Traps
- Rubber Bands
- Those unpopped kernels at the bottom of microwave popcorn

"Eugene," said Stan, "it's amazing you're not allergic to yourself."

"Well, I go back and get tested again next year," said Eugene with a laugh. "So who knows?"

Just then, Stan saw his brother up front in the third row. His eyes widened. He ran up to him. "You can't sit there!" Stan said to Stinky. "That's Penelope's seat!"

"I know," Stinky replied with a sly grin. Then he got up and headed toward the back of the bus.

Although Stinky was usually quiet around his classmates, he could concoct some pretty elaborate plans. Behind the hair that often hung in his eyes, Stinky was one smart and clever eight-year-old.

As Stinky sat down in the back row, the one and only Penelope Parsnippity boarded the bus.

She stopped and flipped her blond hair over her shoulder. Stan thought she actually stopped to pose for just a moment, but he couldn't swear to it.

Right behind Penelope were Tiffanie Flitini and Steffanie Gutierrez. They were Penelope-wanna-bes. Apparently, to be a popular girl, your first name had to end in an "e."

They headed toward their seats in the third row.

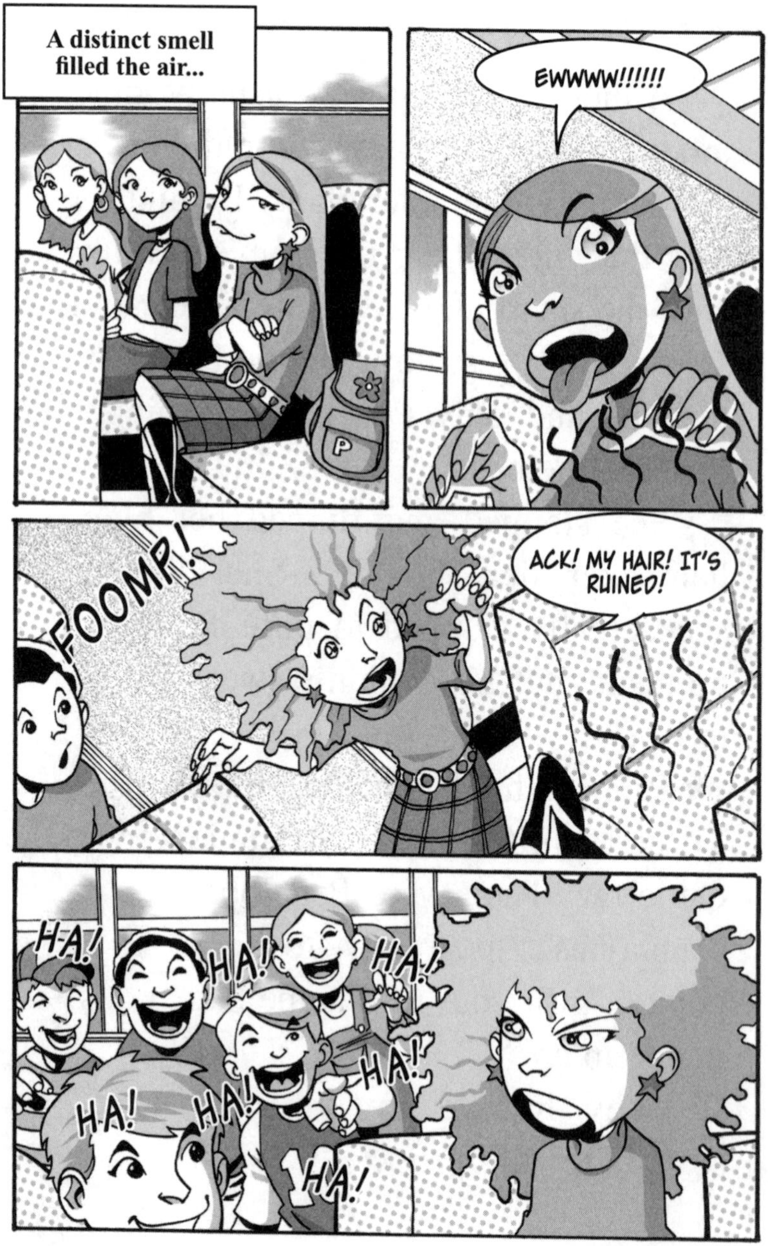
A distinct smell filled the air...
EWWWW!!!!!!
FOOMP!
ACK! MY HAIR! IT'S RUINED!
HA!
HA!
HA!
HA!
HA!
HA!
HA!

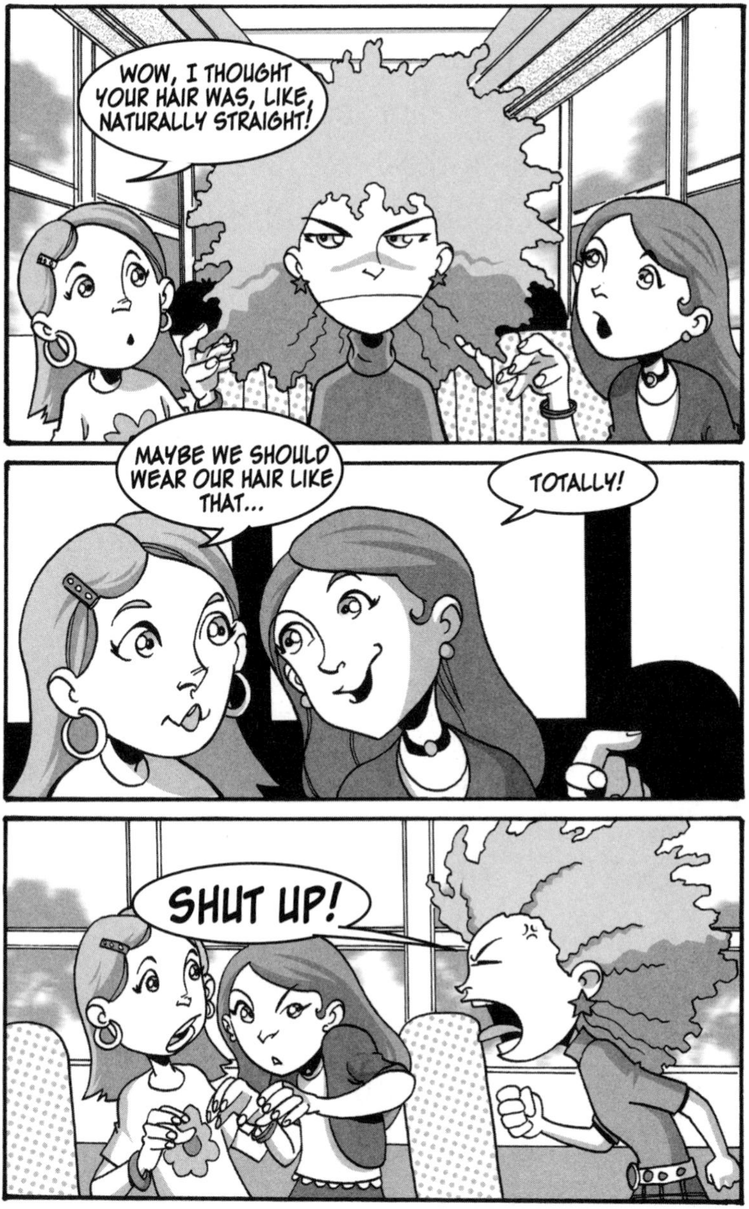
WOW, I THOUGHT YOUR HAIR WAS, LIKE, NATURALLY STRAIGHT!
MAYBE WE SHOULD WEAR OUR HAIR LIKE THAT...
TOTALLY!
SHUT UP!

And what, you may ask, caused Penelope—and her hair—to spring up like a jack-in-the-box? Well, I'll give you a hint: it has to do with a certain boy named Stinky. You see, when Stinky sat there, he *farted*.

Now I'm not talking about a small little *toot*. Stinky's farts were silent but violent. Bad cheese? Bad breath? Bad poopy diaper? These are nothing compared to Stinky's farts.

When he farts, you won't hear it, but you will certainly smell it. One sniff and you'll want to trade in your nose for a new model.

Not to be outdone by his brother, Stan's farts were loud and proud. Stan could fart loud enough to be heard around the world. Well, maybe not that far. But at least halfway.

Together, these fraternal twins had farts that could rule a nation, or at least make fourth-grade a little more challenging for everyone with a nose (except Eugene, who couldn't smell a thing).

Now where were we? Oh, yes, darling, dear Penelope and her oh-so-frizzy hair.

Penelope whipped her head around and glared at Stinky in the back row.

Stinky could have sworn he saw daggers coming out of her eyes.

"Miss Mulch!" whined Penelope, holding her nose. "The smell!"

Miss Mulch sighed. She knew that only one person could be responsible. "Stinky Grosse," she called. "Have you been fart—, uh, sitting up here?"

Stinky didn't want to lie, so he tried to avoid answering the question. "Who, me?" he replied as innocently as he could.

But Miss Mulch knew better. No one else could cause such an odor. "You will apologize to Penelope and then come up here and sit next to me," Miss Mulch instructed.

"Aw, man!" said Stinky, heading toward the front of the bus.

"Sorry," Stinky mumbled to Penelope.

"You should be," Penelope replied.

Then she flipped her frizzy hair and turned away, ordering Steffanie to move so she could take her seat.

Stinky sat down next to Miss Mulch. As much as Stinky didn't want to sit next to the teacher, imagine how Miss Mulch felt!

Let's just say it was going to be a very, very, *very* long ride to the Science Museum.

CHAPTER THREE

THE PUKERATOR

Forty-five minutes later, the bus pulled into the Science Museum parking lot. The kids were excited and piled off the bus. Stinky, Stan, Eugene, and Grñpæk walked toward the entrance.

"I can't believe you did that to Penelope," Stan said to Stinky. "I don't think I've ever been more proud to be your brother."

Stinky laughed. "It *was* pretty cool.

But I can't believe I had to sit next to Miss Mulch the whole way."

"But wasn't it worth it just to see Penelope's reaction?" asked Stan.

"Yeah," Stinky admitted. "Not to mention her hair."

"Oh! My hair! It's ruined!" said Stan, doing his best imitation of Penelope.

"I still don't see what the big deal is," said Eugene. "I can't smell a thing when you fart."

"You're lucky," said Grñpæk. At least that's what they thought he said. To the other boys it sounded like "Brpzlf evvvtzk."

The boys entered the Science Museum. It was filled with lots of cool stuff.

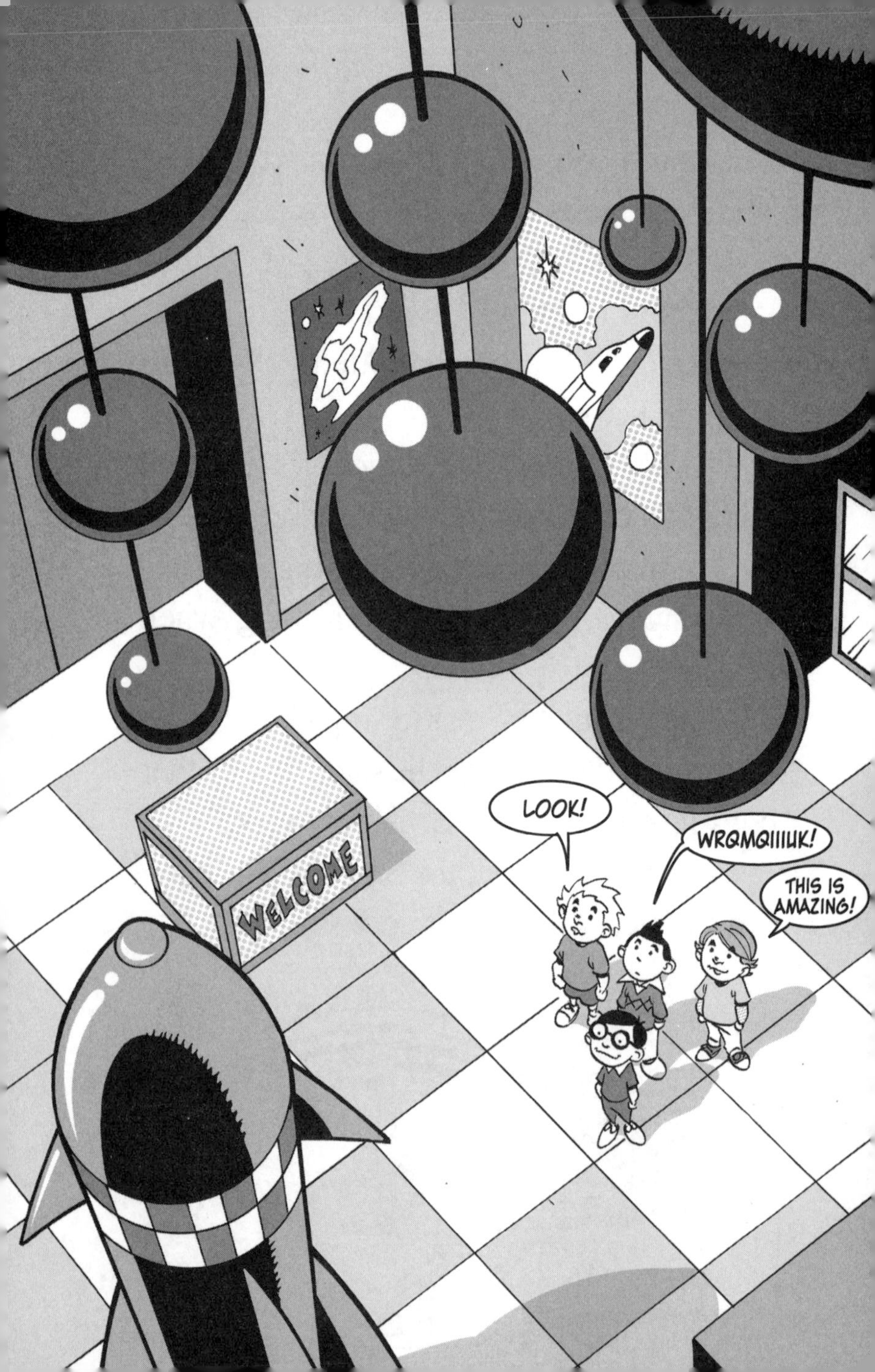
LOOK!
WRQMQIIIUK!
THIS IS AMAZING!
WELCOME

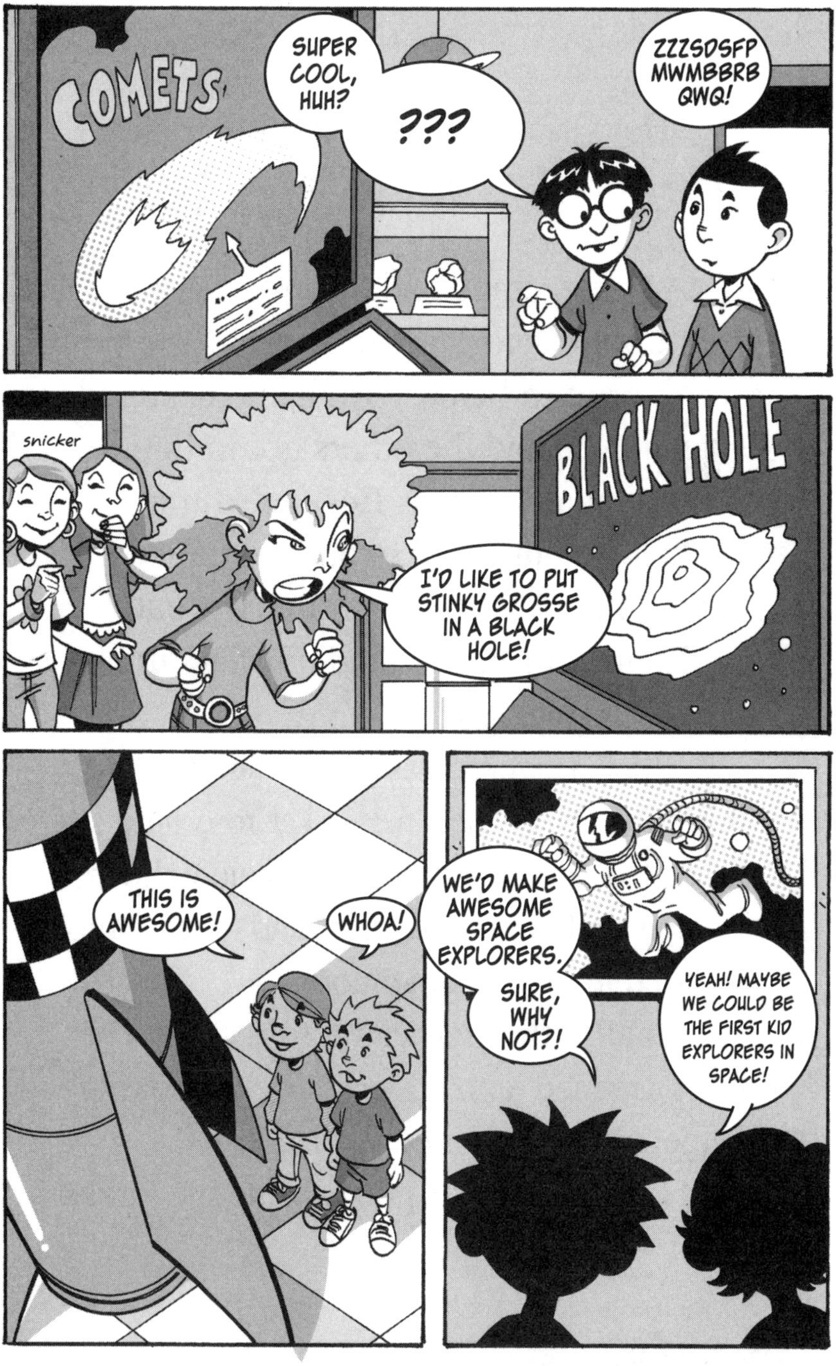
COMETS
SUPER COOL, HUH?
???
ZZZSDSFP MWMBBRB QWQ!
snicker
BLACK HOLE
I'D LIKE TO PUT STINKY GROSSE IN A BLACK HOLE!
THIS IS AWESOME!
WHOA!
WE'D MAKE AWESOME SPACE EXPLORERS.
SURE, WHY NOT?!
YEAH! MAYBE WE COULD BE THE FIRST KID EXPLORERS IN SPACE!

"Hey," said Eugene, pointing. "This looks super fun!" He ran toward a nearby exhibit.

A flight simulator.

"Cool!" said Stan joining him.

"I want to be an astronaut," declared Eugene. He and the others got in line.

Eventually, it was Eugene's turn.

"Good luck, Astronaut Eugene," called Stan. "Make our country proud."

Eugene turned around, puffed out his chest, and saluted.

When Eugene was safely strapped in, the door shut. Then the rocket rose up . . . it jostled around, it turned upside down, it spun and spun and spun and—yes, you guessed it—spun some more.

Finally, the ride came to a stop. The door opened and a very green-looking Eugene slowly exited the ride.

"I don't feel so good," Eugene said.

"I think I'm allergic to space."

Just then, Miss Mulch said the worst thing Eugene could imagine hearing: "Lunchtime!"

CHAPTER FOUR

ALL'S FAIR IN LUNCH AND WAR

In a grassy courtyard, the kids spread out to eat their lunches.

"Hey, Eugene," said Stinky. "Want half of my sandwich?"

"Ugh! Please don't mention food," Eugene replied, still looking queasy from his trip on the flight simulator.

Well, that was all Stan needed to hear. He just couldn't help himself. Teasing Eugene was like an itch he had to scratch.

"Hey, Eugene, do you want my apple?" asked Stan. "Or do you want my banana? Or how about a piece of my cookie? Hey, Eugene—"

But Eugene wasn't there. He was making a beeline straight for the bathroom.

The boys roared with laughter. Stan never passed up an opportunity to joke around and make people laugh.

"I'm going to get a soda," Stinky said to the others. "Be right back."

Stinky went over to the soda machine and got in line. He dug into his pockets for some change.

Meanwhile, at the front of the line, Penelope dropped her money into the machine and pushed down one of the buttons. A can of soda tumbled out. She quickly picked it up, gave a wicked smile, and turned around.

Then Penelope walked by the kids who were waiting in line and went right up to Stinky.

"Oh, no!" cried Penelope, in her most innocent voice. "I must have pushed the wrong button."

She looked at Stinky, who then managed to blush, despite his best efforts not to.

Penelope handed the can of soda to Stinky. "I only drink diet," she said to him. "Do you want it?"

"Uh . . . thanks," Stinky mumbled. He cautiously handed her his soda money as a trade . . .

AW, MAN!

FBBBTH!

HAHAHAHA!

OOPS! SORRY! GUESS IT GOT A LITTLE SHOOK UP!

HEY, WHAT HAPPENED? WHAT'D I MISS?

CHAPTER FIVE

BEANS AGAIN?

"Boys! Patty!" called Mrs. Grosse. "It's dinner time!"

"Coming!" shouted Stinky.

"Be right there!" called Stan.

The boys were just finishing up their homework.

Okay, not really. Stan was reading his favorite manga, *The Adventures of Paste Man*, and Stinky was figuring out whether or not Einstein's theory of relativity really was $E=mc^2$.

As the boys headed out of their room, they ran into Patty, their older sister.

"Well, well," said Patty, "if it isn't Tweedledumb and Tweedledumber."

"Well, well," said Stinky, "if it isn't their even dumber sister."

Patty gave Stinky the evil eye.

Stan gestured for Patty to go down the stairs first. "Age before beauty," he teased.

"Oh, you're so clever, little brother," Patty replied sarcastically. "Did you think of that yourself? Or did it take both of your brains to think that one up?"

"Don't be jealous of us, Sis," said Stan. "It's so unflattering."

"That's it!" Patty ran down the stairs. "Mom! Stan hit me!"

"Stan, don't hit your sister," Mrs. Grosse warned.

"I didn't hit her!" Stan yelled running down the stairs after Patty.

"Stop your fighting and sit down," Mrs. Grosse told them.

Sheila Grosse was a cheerful woman with a kind heart, which was a good thing because she was a pediatrician. She even gave you *two* lollipops if you didn't cry when you got your shots.

"Dinner's going to get cold. Now where is your father?" she asked.

"I'll get him," Stinky offered, and headed toward the den. On the way, he nearly collided with Columbus, the dog, who was chasing after a dust bunny.

Somehow, Columbus was outsmarted by the dust bunny, and he tripped over his own feet and slammed into the wall.

Don't worry, he wasn't hurt. The walls in the Grosse home had a lot of doggy dents in them.

Once Stinky made sure that Columbus was fine, he went into the den. "Dad?" he called. "Dinner's rea—Whoa! What in the world is *that*?"

Stinky pointed to an insect his father was holding. It was one of the ugliest bugs Stinky had ever seen. Imagine the worst cockroach you can. Now add a bunch of antennae. Now pile on a ton of creepy-crawly legs.

Well, this creature was even uglier than that!

"Stinky! Come here!" said Mr. Grosse, excitedly. "Look at this amazing insect! It's extremely rare."

Sheldon Grosse was an entomologist. That's someone who studies insects. His den was covered with cases and cases of specimens. There were insects from Africa and Australia and everywhere in between.

"It's the bug I named *you* after," Mr. Grosse said, showing off the unique insect. "It's called a *Stinkerus Odormoderpoderloderdodera.*"

"Come on, Dad," said Stinky. "I think we know why you named me Stinky."

His father gave Stinky a blank look.

"Because of the farting?" reminded Stinky.

"Actually, the farting was a surprise to us," replied Mr. Grosse. "Originally, since you were twins, Mom and I decided that we'd each get to name one of you kids: Mom got to name Stan, and I got to name you."

"Dad, you named me after an *insect?!*" Stinky exclaimed.

"That's right," replied Mr. Grosse. "Consider yourself lucky. Not all boys are named after such rare specimens."

"Yeah, 'lucky,' " said Stinky. "That's just the word that comes to mind."

"Dinner!" Mrs. Grosse called again.

Stinky and his father went into the dining room and sat down with the family for dinner.

Mrs. Grosse had made one of her

specialties: Tater Tot Tuna and Beans.

"Yum! Beans again!" Stan said and began to eat everything on his plate.

"Yuck! Beans again?" Patty whined.

"They're good for you," said Mrs. Grosse.

Patty grumbled. "Not in *this* family, they're not." She glared at her brothers.

"Now, now," said Mrs. Grosse. "You know I ate beans every day when I was pregnant with Stinky and Stan," Mrs. Grosse said.

"That's right," agreed Mr. Grosse. "She'd make me get up at three in the morning to make her baked beans with bean curd and a side of black beans."

"And sometimes lima bean pie for dessert," reminded Mrs. Grosse, lovingly.

"Yeah," Patty added. "And now *I* have to live with the farts."

"Mom says it's a special gift," Stan reminded her.

"Why can't I have a *normal* family?" Patty wondered aloud.

"There's no such thing as 'normal,' " said Stinky.

"Yeah, *you're* living proof," said Patty.

"And you're living up to your name, *Bratty Patty!*" Stinky shot back.

"That's enough, you two," warned Mrs. Grosse. "No fighting at the dinner table. Now, how was your day, boys?" she asked, trying to change the subject. "How was the Science Museum?"

"It was awesome!" said Stan.

"Yeah," chimed in Stinky, helping himself to more beans. "We saw a cool meteorite and a rocket and a display on the planets—"

"—and then Eugene got sick from going on this flight simulator ride," added Stan.

"Oh, that poor dear!" said Mrs. Grosse.

"Did you know that there have been insects in space?" Mr. Grosse said.

"Oh, great. We've gone from beans to farts to bugs," said Patty, rolling her eyes. "Could this get any worse?"

Just then, Stinky and Stan exchanged a quick look. It was time for the *Double Booty Bomber!*

Stinky let out a smelly fart and Stan let out a loud fart—at exactly the same time. It was quite overwhelming! The wallpaper in the room peeled away from the wall and the windows fogged up.

Even Columbus had to cover his nose with his paws.

"*Eww!*" said Patty, covering her nose. "It *did* get worse!"

Stinky and Stan high-fived each other.

Mr. and Mrs. Grosse put their napkins over their noses. They were used to this.

Once the smell died down, Mrs. Grosse cleared her throat. "Now what do we say?" she asked. She loved her sons, but manners were important.

"Excuse me," said Stan.

"Excuse me," said Stinky.

Mrs. Grosse nodded her approval. "Now who wants dessert? I've made some delicious vanilla and kidney bean ice cream from scratch."

CHAPTER SIX

PROJECT: BEAT PENELOPE

Miss Mulch stood in front of the classroom. "I hope you all enjoyed the Science Museum yesterday, because it's time to start the projects for the Fourth Grade Astronomy Fair."

The class reaction was mixed:

"Cool!"

"Yuck!"

"Do we have to?"

"Neat!"

"Wzzqpömrbm!"

"You may take a few minutes to pick out your project partners," Miss Mulch instructed.

The class milled around and began to pair up. Stinky and Stan decided to be a team. Eugene took Grñpæk as his partner.

Penelope had a hard choice to make: she had to choose between Tiffanie and Steffanie.

"Pick me!" said Tiffanie.

"No! Pick me!" said Steffanie.

"I'll let you borrow my new lip gloss," said Tiffanie.

Steffanie had to think fast (which of course was a challenging thing for her to do).

"I'll let you borrow my new Pink Bubblegum nail polish," she offered to Penelope.

In reality, it didn't matter much whom Penelope chose as her partner, since she would end up doing most of the work anyway. Penelope was a smart girl—the smartest in the class. Too bad she was so snobby.

Suddenly, Tiffanie pulled out all the stops . . .

"I'll let you borrow all my Boy Band, Inc. CDs," said Tiffanie.

Penelope smiled slightly. "I choose Tiffanie," she announced.

"Yay!" cheered Tiffanie.

Steffanie sighed heavily. "I, like, can't believe I didn't get picked. This is, like, totally uncool," she said and went to find another partner.

Soon after, the bell rang.

As the kids poured out of the classroom, Penelope approached Stinky and Stan.

"So, what's your project going to be?" said Penelope. "How To Make a Nerd-O-Meter?"

"Good one, Penelope," said Tiffanie with a giggle.

"Ha. Ha," replied Stan.

"There's no need to try very hard, because *my* project is going to win," Penelope told the boys.

"Yeah, *our* project is going to win," added Tiffanie.

"You wish," said Stan.

"Well, you're used to losing, so I'm sure you'll feel right at home," said Penelope.

That's when Stan snapped. He just couldn't take it anymore.

"Oh, yeah?" he said. "Well, our project will blow you away. We're going to build . . . uh . . ." He looked down at the cover of his science book. "We're going to build a rocket!"

Stinky looked over at his brother, confused. "We are?"

Penelope raised an eyebrow. "Good luck," she said snottily. "You'll definitely need it."

"Yeah," was all Tiffanie could think of to add, as she trailed behind Penelope.

After the girls left, Stinky turned to Stan. "What was that?" he asked.

"Penelope thinks she's going to win. But not this time!" said Stan.

"But she's won everything since kindergarten," Stinky pointed out.

"Well, times are about to change," declared Stan. "The Grosse brothers are about to make history!"

"Or go down trying . . ." Stinky added nervously.

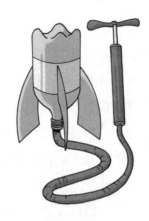

CHAPTER SEVEN

COUNTDOWN TO TROUBLE

"How are we going to build a rocket?" Stinky asked Stan. They were at home in their room.

"Trust me," said Stan. "I know we can do this."

"Us and what team of scientists?" replied Stinky. He was mad at Stan for bragging to Penelope. "You shouldn't have said that we were going to build a rocket."

"Look," said Stan. "We're smart. We can do this. The rocket doesn't have to go into outer space, it just has to be good enough to beat Penelope's project."

Stinky couldn't argue with that. "Okay, but next time, check with me before you turn us into NASA engineers."

"You know," said Stan, "we could ask Miss Mulch if we could change the project."

"And let Penelope have the last laugh?" replied Stinky. "Not a chance."

Stan grinned. He was glad Stinky was now on board with the project.

"Let's get started!" Stinky said.

"Internet?" suggested Stan.

"Sure," said Stinky, "but we'd better go to the library, too. Remember that website we found that quoted Paul Revere saying 'The British *aren't* coming'?"

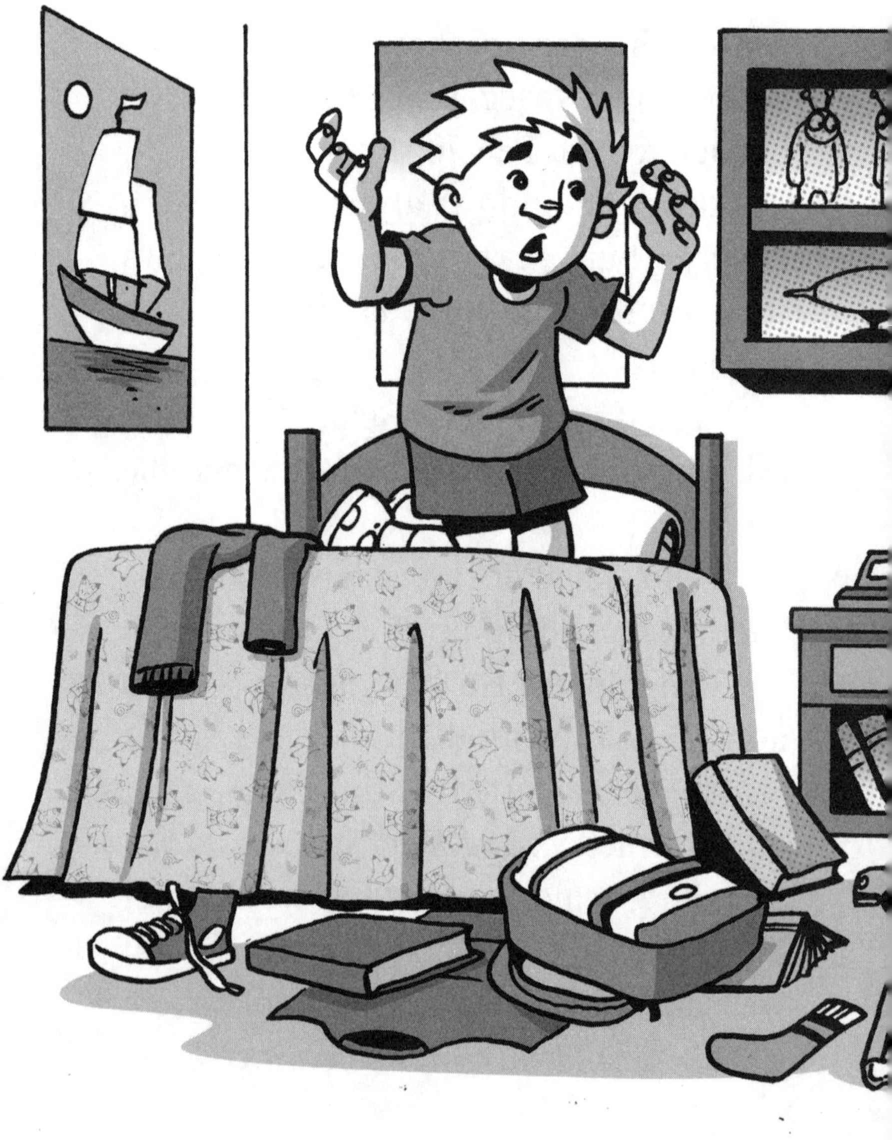

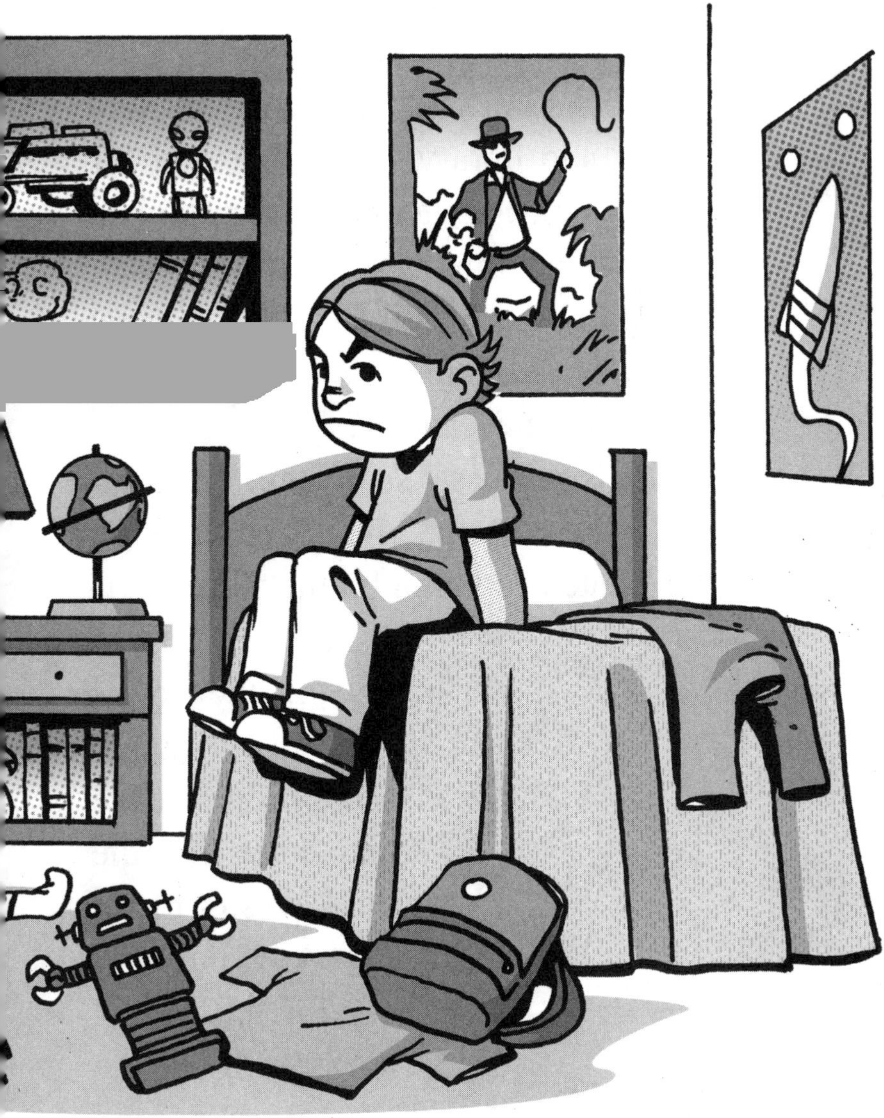

"Oh, yeah," said Stan. "Good point. Let's start at the library."

The boys got on their bikes and rode to the public library. They searched for books in the computer catalog system.

"Look at this one," said Stinky, pointing to an entry on the screen. *"How To Build a Rocket for a Fourth Grade Astronomy Fair—and Win."*

"That's perfect," said Stan. "And no one's checked it out," he added, looking in the "status" column on the screen.

Excited by this news, the boys headed to the book section on science and space. But the book wasn't there.

"Are you looking for this?" said a snobbish voice.

The boys turned to see Penelope . . . holding the book they needed.

"Give it," said Stan, sticking out his hand.

"Why should I?" replied Penelope.

"You're not even doing a rocket project," Stan pointed out.

"That doesn't mean I have to make it easy for you," Penelope said.

"Does being mean come naturally to you?" Stan asked.

"Only around goobers like you," Penelope replied, with a smug smile.

While this was all happening, Stinky stayed quiet. He was working on a plan of his own, and it was just about to go into action . . .

"Hey, look!" Stinky called out, pointing behind Penelope. "It's that guy Brandon from Boy Band, Inc.!"

"Huh?" Penelope said and turned her head to look.

Stinky grabbed the rocket book.

"Run!" he called to Stan.

The boys ran to the counter, checked out the book, and made it out the door before Penelope even knew what had happened.

"All right!" the boys said, giving each other a high five.

"Let's go build a rocket!" exclaimed Stan.

The boys went home and immediately began to read *How To Build a Rocket for a Fourth Grade Astronomy Fair—and Win*. They gathered what they would need and then checked off the list of the necessary items to make the rocket.

"Cork?" Stinky read off the list.

"Check," replied Stan, looking at the cork in their pile of items.

"Plastic bottle?"

"Check."

"Bicycle pump?"

"Check."

"Balsa wood for the stand?"

"Check."

"Glue?"

"Check."

"Banana?"

"Huh?!"

"Just seeing if you were paying attention," said Stinky, laughing.

They looked to make sure they had the rest of the items on the list.

"We're ready," said Stan. "Let's do it."

The boys asked their dad to cut out the balsa wood for the stand that the rocket would be placed in. Then they filled the bottle with water and assembled the other pieces into place.

They headed to the backyard so their rocket wouldn't blow a hole in the roof . . . or worse.

Stinky and Stan stood far away from the rocket, just in case. Stan began to use the bicycle pump.

The pressure began to build and build. When it reached breaking point, the rocket would propel into the air.

The countdown began: Five . . . four . . . three . . . two . . .

Just then Columbus came sniffing around.

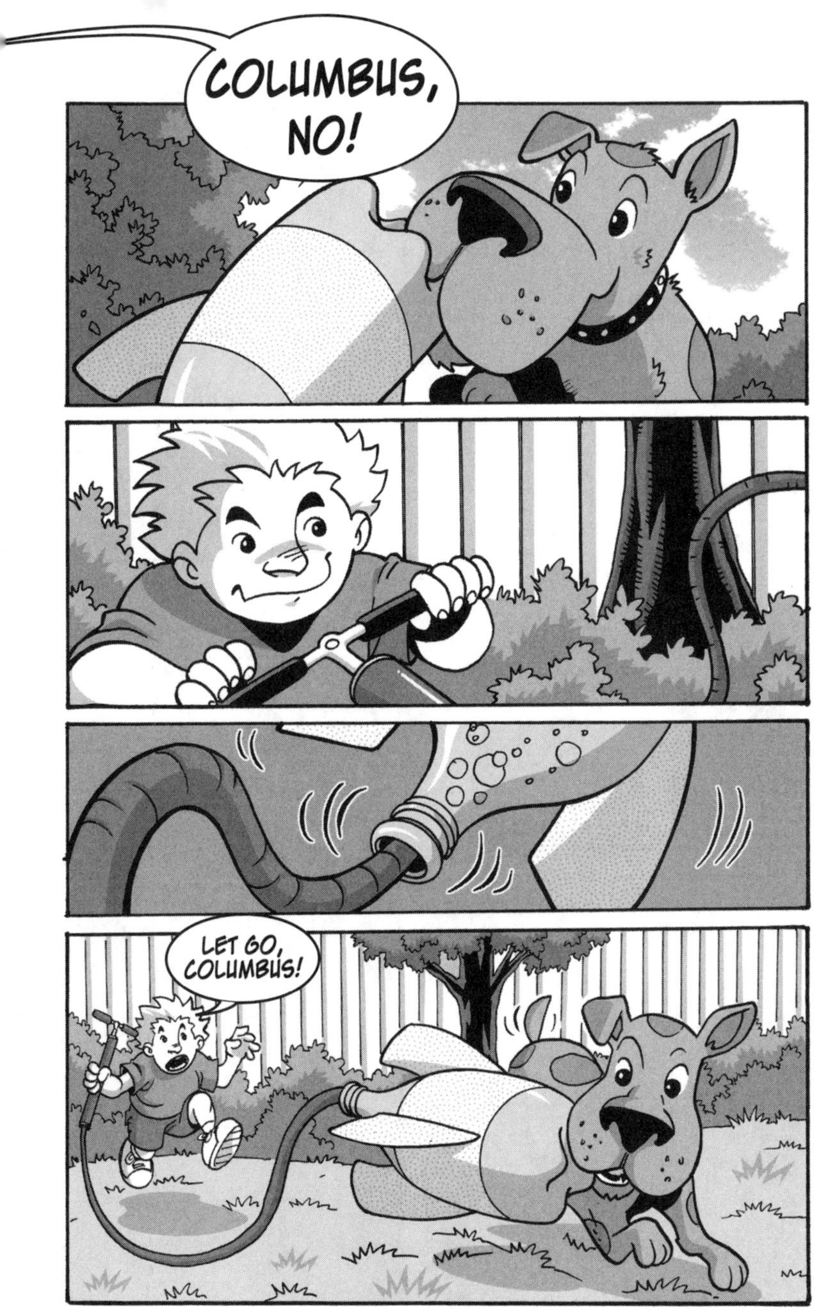
COLUMBUS, NO!
LET GO, COLUMBUS!

Would the rocket ever land?

CHAPTER EIGHT

DAD TO THE RESCUE

Finally the rocket touched down . . . into a pile of leaves their dad had just raked.

Columbus ran over to the pile of leaves and grabbed the rocket in his mouth.

Stinky and Stan rushed over.

"Sorry, Dad," said Stinky.

"Yeah, sorry, Dad," said Stan.

"What's going on?" Mr. Grosse asked his sons.

"Columbus messed up our school project," explained Stinky.

Columbus rolled over, trying to look cute. Then he shook himself off and trotted away with the piece of the rocket still in his mouth.

He seemed to be perfectly fine.

"Columbus! Come back here now!" shouted Stan. "That's not a chew toy!"

"Aw, man! What are we going to do?" wondered Stinky. "Our project is due tomorrow. And we'll *never* get that piece back from Columbus."

"What are we going to tell Miss Mulch? That our dog really ate our homework?" Stan said.

"Now we have no chance of winning the Astronomy Fair," Stinky said disappointedly.

"Couldn't you build another one?" suggested their father.

"Columbus might take pieces from that, too," Stinky answered. He frowned. "I bet NASA never had its rocket parts eaten by a dog."

"Hmm," said Mr. Grosse. "It sounds like you need a rocket that Columbus can't chew through."

"Yeah," said Stan, looking glum. "Got any metal pieces stashed in your pile of leaves, Dad?"

"No," replied Mr. Grosse. "But I could take you to the scrap yard if you want."

The boys' faces lit up.

"That'd be awesome!" said Stan.

"Yeah," agreed Stinky. "The metal will make our rocket look *really* cool!"

The boys piled into the car with their father and headed for the scrap yard. It was located at the other end of Burbsburg.

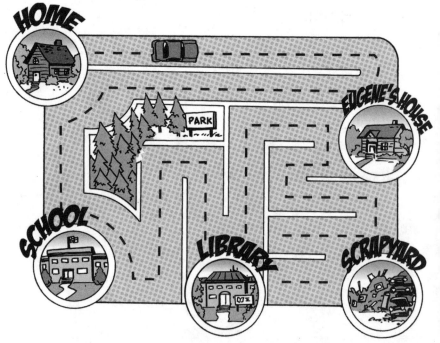

There, they searched through old cars, old kitchen appliances, and what looked like old time machines.

"This place is cool!" said Stan.

"Yeah!" agreed Stinky. "We're definitely going to have to come back here and go exploring!"

"Hurry up, boys," called Mr. Grosse. "It's starting to get dark."

The boys ran around and gathered up as many metal pieces as they could carry. A few minutes later, they were back in the car, heading home.

"Thanks, Dad," said Stinky. "This stuff is great!"

Back home, the family gathered around the table. The boys hurriedly ate dinner—another of Sheila Grosse's "unique" recipes: Chicken and Brussels Sprouts Surprise. The boys didn't care how it tasted; they just wanted to finish and get started on their project.

They worked in the garage where there was light, and assembled a new rocket. They decided to build one just like the one they had built earlier. Then they would add its protective metal covering.

Just then, Columbus poked his head in the garage. He sniffed the air and barked. *Ruff!*

"Columbus, go away!" yelled Stinky.

As Columbus slinked away, Stan said, "All right. It's metal time!"

With some duct tape, glue, wire, and even some chewing gum, Stinky and Stan attached the metal pieces to their rocket. They painted an insect on the side to honor their father and his help.

"Hey, let's put a letter inside in case it goes up into space," suggested Stinky.

"Good thinking, Stink," said Stan. He grabbed some paper and a marker and wrote a short note.

Dear Aliens,
Hi. How are you?
If you find this
rocket, please return to:
Stinky & Stan Grosse
2727 Makenmegag Rd.
Burbsburg
        Earth

Suddenly, Patty came into the garage. "What are you dweebs doing?"

"We're building a rocket," explained Stan.

"For the Astronomy Fair tomorrow," added Stinky.

"You started your project the night before?" Patty asked. "That's *really* smart."

Stinky gritted his teeth. "It's a long story."

"Yeah, and all we have to do is test it," said Stan. "So if you don't mind leaving—"

"Where are you going to test a rocket?" said Patty. "It's dark outside."

Stinky and Stan looked at each other. They *hated* when Patty was right.

Patty snickered. "Well, I'll leave you two Einsteins to figure this out. I'll see ya."

After she left, Stinky turned to Stan and said, "I guess we're not going to have time to test the new rocket."

Stan tried to look on the bright side. "Well, the rocket worked last time, and we just have a *few* more parts on it this time. What could go wrong?"

CHAPTER NINE

AND THE WINNER IS . . .

Finally, the day of the Fourth Grade Astronomy Fair had arrived. Excitement buzzed around the school.

Well, actually, the fifth and sixth graders couldn't care less. But the fourth graders were all a-twitter!

Miss Mulch, Principal Dingle, and Mrs. Garrett the Lunch Lady were the judges. Each pair of students would have a few minutes to explain their astronomy projects to the judges and the other students.

The students' projects were all very different. There were projects on meteors, Mars, and the moon. There were projects dealing with stars, the sun, and the entire solar system. There were projects that ranged from good to bad . . . to very, very bad.

The first presenters were Tiffanie and her partner, Kim-Yun. They made styrofoam models of the solar system.

But the planets looked more like giant spitballs instead.

Eugene and Grñpæk gave their presentation next. Eugene made the decision that he would be the one to do the presenting. Smart choice, huh? He also made the decision to call Grñpæk just "G." An even smarter choice.

"This is the one and only Transalienator," explained Eugene. "G and I created this translator so we could communicate with the aliens."

"What aliens are you talking about?" asked Principal Dingle.

"The aliens that will surely come here one day," Eugene said, matter-of-factly.

The other students looked surprised.

Miss Mulch frowned. "And how are you going to demonstrate this 'translator' without any aliens?"

"I've got that all figured out," Eugene reassured her. "G and I will use it so we can understand *each other*. At least until the aliens come, that is."

Miss Mulch looked at the other judges. "All right, show us how it works," she instructed Eugene.

"Certainly," he replied. "G just says something into this mouthpiece and then the machine translates it. Here, we'll show you."

Eugene handed the translator to Grñpæk, who took it and said into the mouthpiece, "Gñvq ptç gvhiyy x lppdeö kljwöb."

The machine translated and read in a robotic voice: "Shoes are tasty when you eat them with seat belts and peanut butter."

The other kids laughed. The judges scribbled on their clipboards.

"Aw, gee!" exclaimed Eugene.

"Mbpp izqxå!" exclaimed Grñpæk.

"Sour clams!" translated the machine.

"I think your translator needs a little work," Miss Mulch said to Eugene and Grñpæk.

Grñpæk looked discouraged.

"Don't worry," Eugene told him. "We'll figure it out."

Then Miss Mulch moved on to the next student team: Stinky and Stan. She looked behind them, but there was nothing there.

"Have you misplaced your project?" she asked the boys.

"No," replied Stan. "But we have to go outside to demonstrate it."

The students and judges followed Stinky and Stan outside to an open area where the boys had set up their rocket. The other kids thought the rocket looked cool. And frankly, it *did* look cool.

Stan was more comfortable talking in front of people, so Stinky suggested that his brother give the speech.

"Thank you all for coming out here to see our rocket—the soon-to-be winner of the Fourth Grade Astronomy Fair," Stan began.

"I doubt that," Penelope said, folding her arms and sneering.

"I'd like to welcome you all to the first Grosse Brothers' Mission. Today, a mere rocket. Tomorrow, we'll blast Penelope to the Moon."

"Stanley!" shouted Miss Mulch.

"Just kidding!" Stan said with a snicker. He cleared his throat and then continued: "Stinky and I felt it was our duty to participate in the search for answers to the universe. It took years of preparation, months of hard work, and hours of testing to build a rocket that would make a giant leap for mankind in the pursuit of—"

"Didn't you learn how to build that rocket from a book?" Penelope interrupted.

"Shh," whispered Stan. "Now, where was I?"

"You were making a giant leap for mankind," Stinky said.

"Oh, right," Stan said. "A giant leap—"

"Enough with the speech," someone called out. "Let's see the rocket take off."

"Yeah! Let's see the rocket go!" other kids agreed.

"All right, all right," said Stan. "But remember: do *not* try this at home."

Stinky and Stan walked over to the bicycle pump.

"Think it'll work?" Stinky whispered nervously to Stan.

"There's only one way to find out!" replied Stan.

Five . . . four . . . three . . . two . . . one . . . But the rocket just gave a weak little sputter, went up about two inches, and then fell to the ground.

"What happened?" exclaimed Stan.

"Oh, no! It failed!" exclaimed Stinky.

The boys ran to the rocket and tried to figure out what went wrong. The judges and the other students began to head back inside.

"It'll just be a second," Stan assured the judges, trying to get them to stay. "I'm sure we'll have it working in a minute."

Through a slit in the metal, Stinky saw that the plastic bottle was crushed.

"It looks like the metal is too heavy," he whispered to Stan. "It can't lift off the ground!"

"This wasn't supposed to happen," said Stan. "This is bad. This is very bad!"

The boys didn't know what to do. They started to panic. And then, well, they were so nervous that they accidentally farted.

As you can imagine, that made everyone else flee back indoors.

Stinky and Stan's project was a disaster!

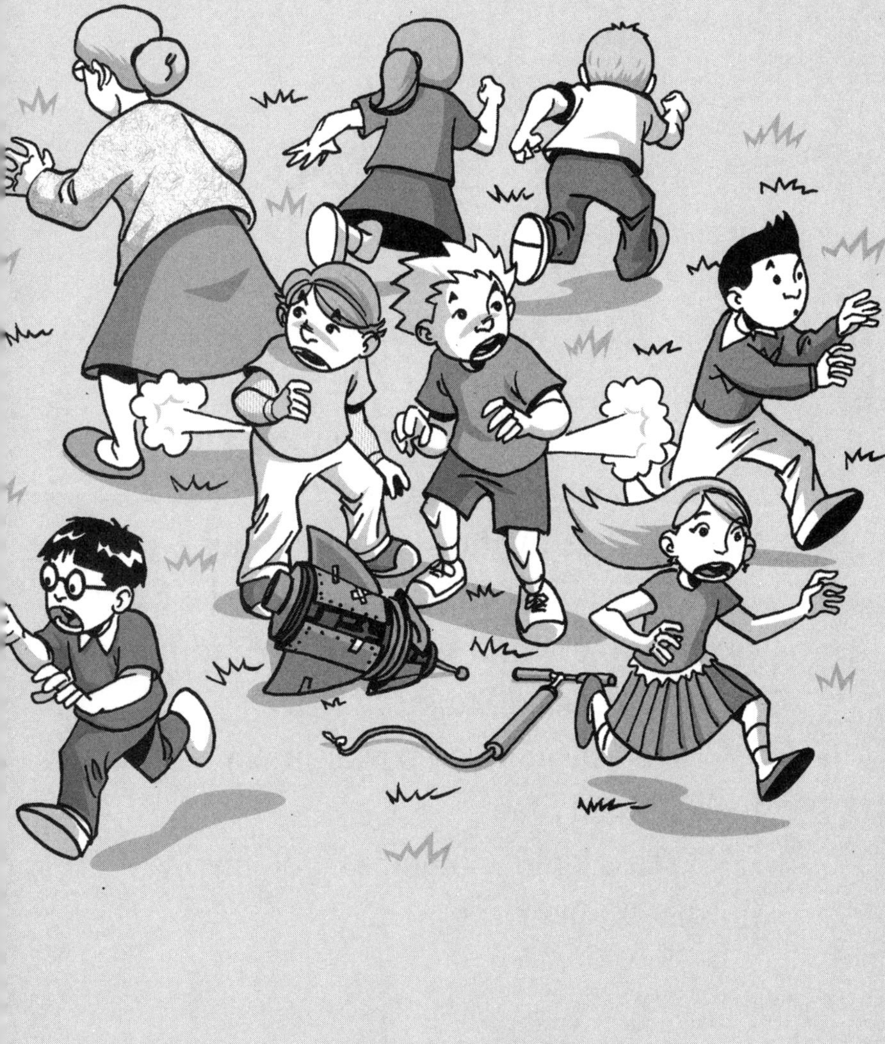

CHAPTER TEN

THE BIG BANG

"What a disaster!" exclaimed Stinky.

"I can't believe it didn't work," said Stan. "All we're left with is a hunk of junk."

"This stinks! I don't think all the extra credit in the world would be able to make up for this," said Stinky.

"We had so much power in our original rocket," said Stan.

"Yeah, until Columbus got involved," finished Stinky.

"And I can't believe we farted, too. I hate it when it happens like that!" complained Stan, kicking a can on the ground.

Suddenly Stinky had an idea!

"Hey, Stan," he said. "Remember that soda can that Penelope shook up and then I opened?"

Stan nodded and said, "You mean the one that exploded all over you, and then it made you all sticky, and then you stuck to the bus seat and Miss Mulch had to pull you off and—"

"Ha, ha. That's enough, wise guy," Stinky interrupted. "Anyway, I was thinking: if the gas bubbles in that soda made it explode all over me, then maybe *our* gas can cause our rocket to fly!"

Stan's face lit up. "That just might work!" he said. "Besides, what have we got to lose?"

"Let's hurry and see if we can make this work while the Astronomy Fair is still going on," said Stinky. "I think we'll have to do the *Double Booty Bomber* to make this work."

"But wait," said Stan. "How are we going to fart into the rocket?"

"Hmmm . . . good question," replied Stinky. He looked around. He spotted a few gopher holes in the ground.

"A-ha!" Stinky exclaimed. He quickly drew a diagram in the dirt to explain his idea to Stan. "It's kind of like fart fuel!"

"Stinky, you're a genius!" declared Stan.

"Yeah, well, it runs in the family," said Stinky.

"And luckily, so does farting!" said Stan with a laugh.

Meanwhile . . .

Penelope and Tiffanie were standing in front of their Mars Rover project. Penelope beamed with pride as she reached out to accept her first place ribbon when suddenly—

BOOM!

"What was that?" asked Principal Dingle.

"Let's go see!" said Eugene.

The kids and judges ran out of the auditorium doors.

"WAIT! Please come back!" cried Penelope. "I have to give my acceptance speech!"

But Penelope and Tiffanie were the only ones left in the auditorium.

"Let's go see what's going on," suggested Tiffanie.

Penelope sighed and they went outside—just in time to see that Stinky and Stan's rocket had taken off!

"Look at it go!" exclaimed Stinky.

"Woo-hoo! It actually worked!" yelled Stan.

The other kids and judges peered into the sky with their mouths hanging open.

"Whoa! It's going into space!!" cried Eugene.

Principal Dingle handed the two first-place ribbons to Stinky and Stan. "Congratulations, boys," he said. "You deserve it."

"Thank you!" replied Stinky and Stan, grinning from ear to ear.

"This is *so* unfair!" Penelope complained.

"Way to go!" hollered Eugene.

"Wxzvvts!" said Grñpæk.

And so, the underdogs became top dogs . . . if only for the afternoon.

BONUS MANGA
JOURNEY TO URANUS

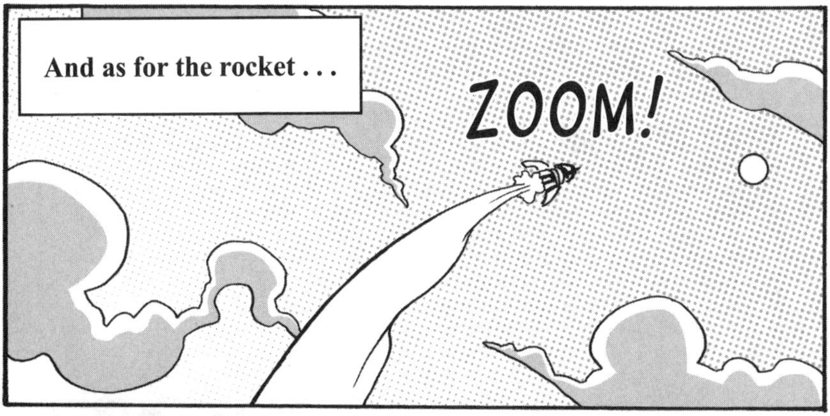
And as for the rocket . . .
ZOOM!

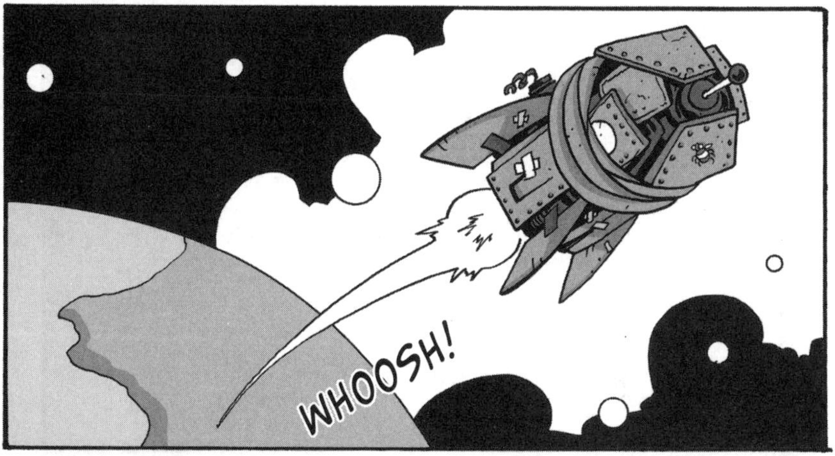
WHOOSH!

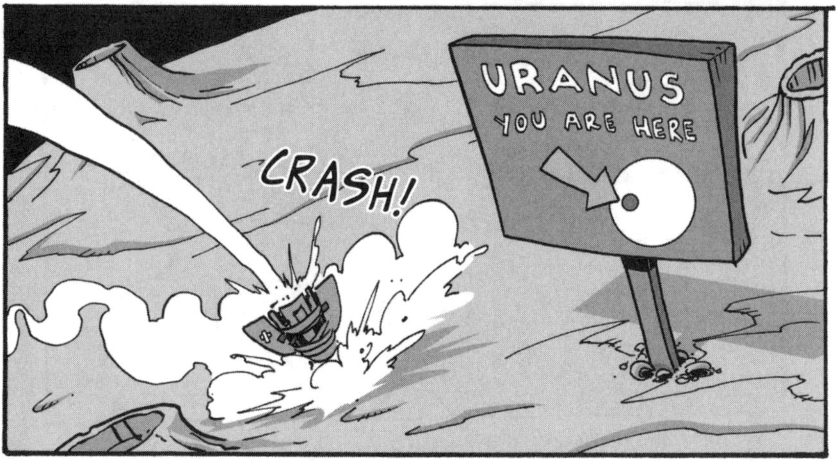
CRASH!
URANUS
YOU ARE HERE

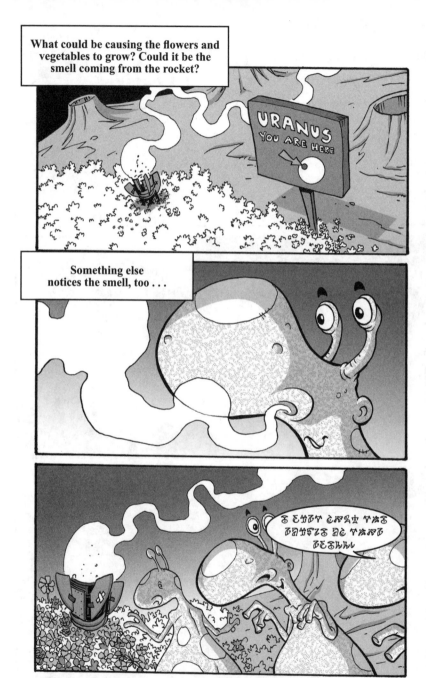

*We must find the source of this smell!

*The smell is coming from the rocket, sir!

*But we must find the original source!

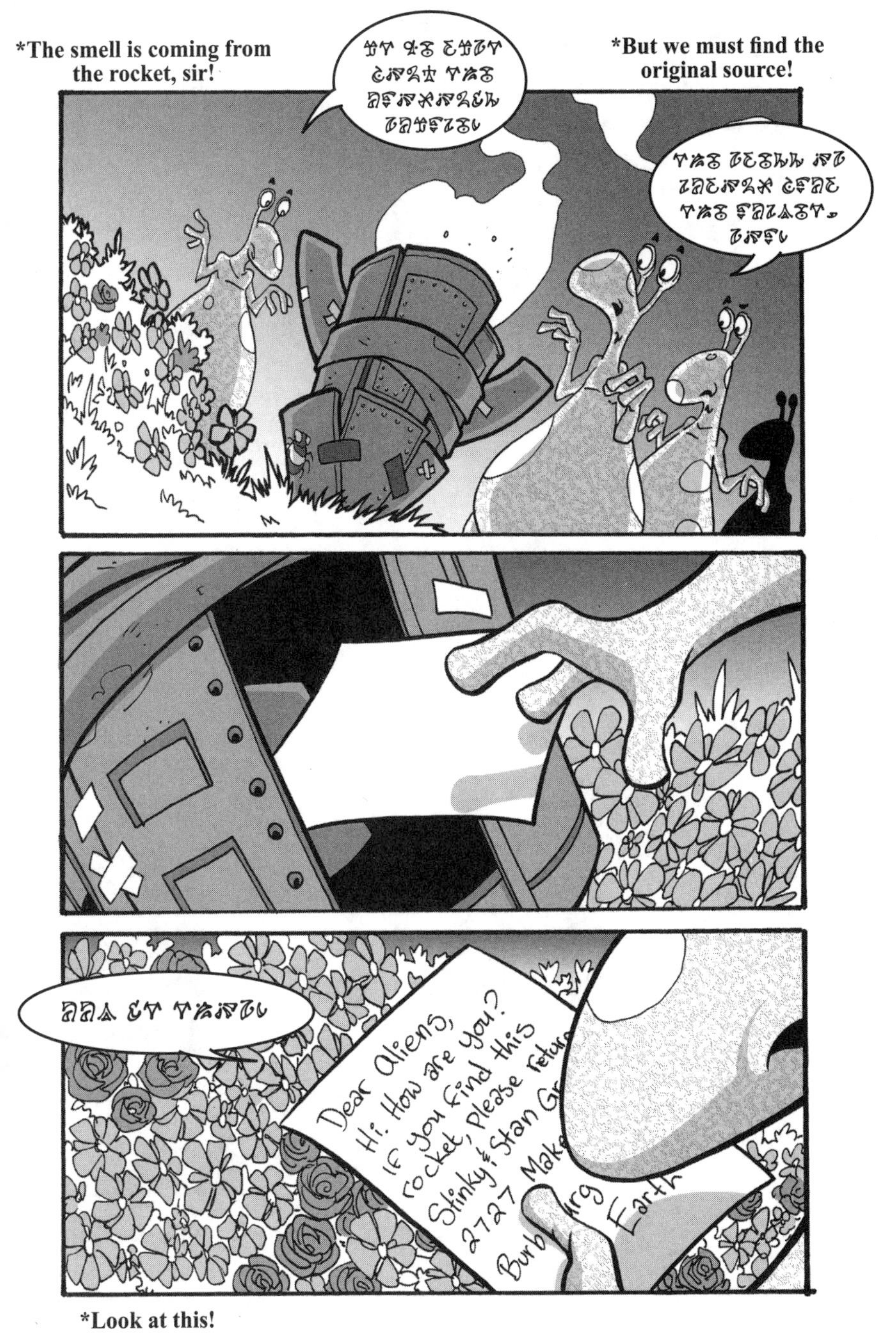
Dear Aliens,
Hi. How are you?
If you find this
rocket, please retur
Stinky, Stan Gr
2727 Make
Burb rg
Earth

*Look at this!

Uh-oh! It looks like Stinky and Stan might get some unexpected visitors . . .

STINKY & STAN BLAST OFF!

**FIND OUT THE ANSWERS TO THESE
QUESTIONS AND MORE AS**

THE GROSSE ADVENTURES CONTINUE ...

1. Will Stinky and Stan receive a visit from the Aliens?

2. Will Eugene ever get the Transalienator to work?

3. Where will Stinky and Stan explore next?

4. What happens when you fart on another planet?

5. Will Patty ever get along with her brothers?

**DON'T MISS THE NEXT BOOK IN
THE GROSSE ADVENTURES SERIES!**